A Gift for Amma

MARKET DAY IN INDIA

WRITTEN BY Meera Sriram

ILLUSTRATED BY Mariona Cabassa

Barefoot Books
Step inside a story

The sun grows bright. The street is busy.
It's market day in town!

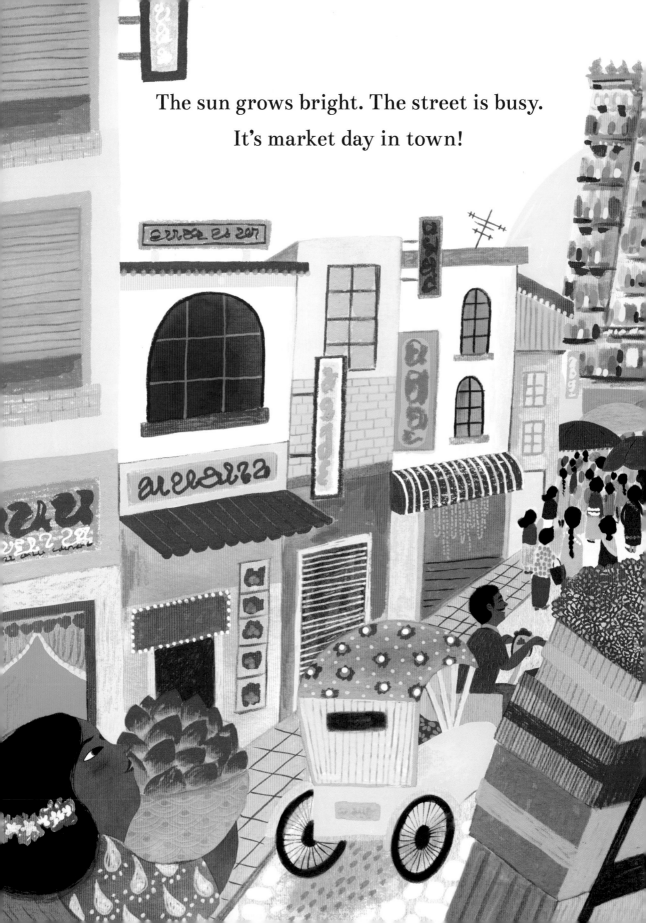

I count my money and dash outside
To find a treasure for Amma.

SAFFRON orange strands in tiny scoops.
Would Amma like to season rice?

Orange marigolds swing over doors —
Swish, swish! Should I make her a garland?

JASMINE white in starry blooms,
Petals to perfume Amma's braid.

But white goats shove past —
Shoo, shoo! I squirm away.

LOTUS pink shimmering fresh.
Would Amma like dewy buds?

Pink sweets soaked in ghee —
Yum, yum! I'll come back for my treat.

PEACOCK green dancing in the breeze...
Would she need a fan for the heat?

Green herbs — mint and coriander —
Sniff, sniff! I'm hungry for chutney.

VERMILION red like rising flame,
But Amma never dots her forehead.

Red-hot peppers spill over —
Achoo, achoo! I cover my face.

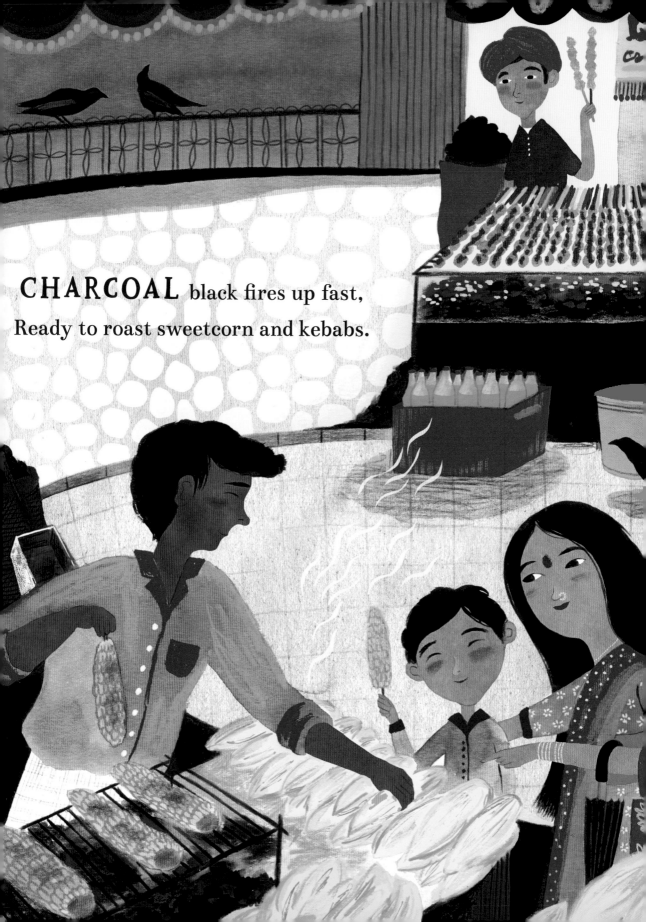

CHARCOAL black fires up fast,
Ready to roast sweetcorn and kebabs.

Black drums beat and boom —
Hop, skip! What would Amma like?

TURMERIC yellow like sunshine dust,
Plenty of powdery spice at home.

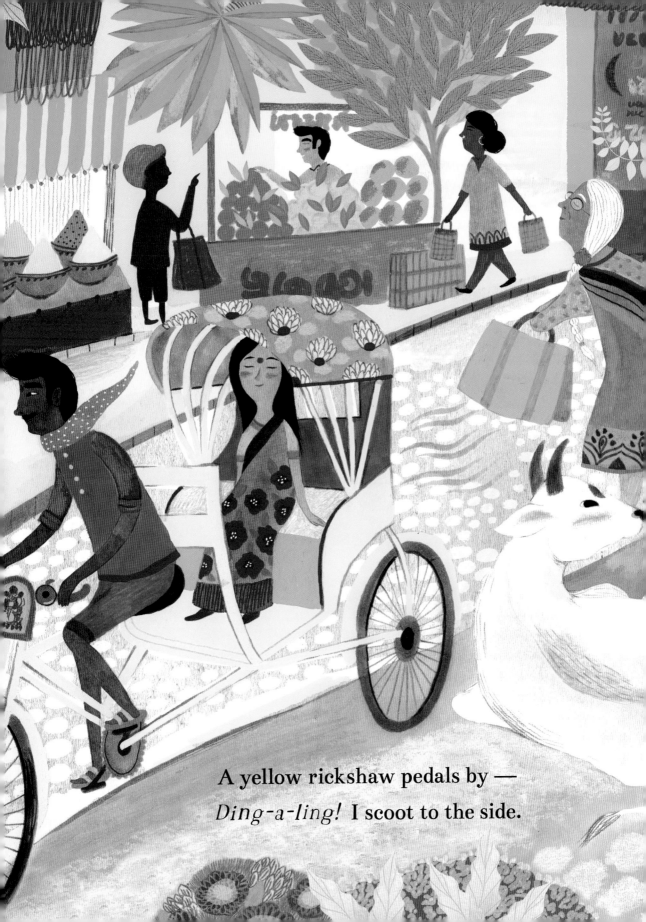

A yellow rickshaw pedals by —
Ding-a-ling! I scoot to the side.

PIGEON grey at every corner,
Street birds pecking grains.

Grey buffalo blinks and stomps —
Moo, moo! I must hurry.

TERRACOTTA brown baked from clay,
Cool water in delicate pots.

Brown tea with milk and sugar —

"*Tea, tea!*" I smell cardamom.

INDIGO blue waves to me,
Soft cotton like Amma's sari.

Blue bangles sing and chime —
Clink, clink! Like Amma's lullaby.

I pick a bangle in every shade
And hand over my pocket money.

I skip back home and tiptoe in.
Jingle, jingle …

. . . a rainbow just for Amma!

What's at the Market?

The market in this story is based on the Vadapalani and Mylapore markets in the author's hometown, Chennai, in India.

SAFFRON: a thin, orange, thread-like part of the crocus flower, used as a spice and dye for food

JASMINE: a sweet-smelling white flower that grows in Asia; worn on the head as decoration

LOTUS: a big pink flower that grows in lakes and ponds; the national flower of India

PEACOCK: a bird with long green tail feathers (only on the males) that open up into a fan shape; the national bird of India

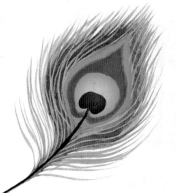

VERMILION: bright red powder that people of the Hindu religion sometimes wear in a dot on their foreheads

CHARCOAL: a kind of half-burnt black wood used to cook corn, meat, bread and other foods outdoors

TURMERIC: a yellow plant root, similar to ginger, used as a medicine and cooking spice

PIGEON: grey, white or speckled bird found almost everywhere on Earth except the driest deserts and the North and South Poles

TERRACOTTA: a brown, baked clay material used to make bricks, pots, cups, toys and artwork

INDIGO: a dark blue fabric dye originally made from plants that grow in India

Markets Around the World

Markets have been around for thousands of years. The earliest markets, called **bazaars,** are thought to have started in the region of Persia (now called Iran).

Marrakech's Souks
(Marrakech, Morocco)

"Souk" (SHOOK) is the Arabic word for "market." In the souks of Marrakech, you can buy clothing, food, artwork and other items from all around the world. At a souk, you might see customers bargaining or "haggling" with the merchants to try to get a lower price.

Kraków Cloth Hall
(Kraków, Poland)

At a cloth hall, you can buy fabric for making clothes, rugs, curtains and other crafts. The Cloth Hall in Kraków (CRACK-oof), built in the 13th century, is considered the world's oldest shopping mall. The buildings and streets are kept to look like they did back in medieval times.

Did you know?

★ The world's **oldest market** is the Grand Bazaar in Istanbul, Turkey.

★ The world's **largest bazaar** is the Bazaar of Tabriz in Tabriz, Iran.

Shilin Night Market
(Shilin District, Taipei, Taiwan)

Night markets are outdoor street markets that are open at night. The Shilin (SHIH-lin) Night Market is famous for its xiaochi (show-chee), which are snack-sized street foods such as stinky tofu, oyster omelettes, pineapple cake and fried ice cream.

Mercado de Jamaica
(Mexico City, Mexico)

Mercado de Jamaica (mer-CAH-doh day ha-MAY-ca) is a flower market. "Jamaica" is the Spanish word for "hibiscus," an important flower in Mexican food and culture. At Mercado de Jamaica, you can visit over a thousand stalls that sell beautiful plants. Most of the stands are open all day and all night long, because it takes a lot of work to care for all those flowers!

Damnoen Saduak Floating Market *(Damnoen Saduak District, Ratchaburi, Thailand)*

People buy and sell things on boats at floating markets, such as the Damnoen Saduak (DAM-noon SAD-oo-ack). Here, you can buy food cooked in a canoe, such as Thailand's famous boat noodles with pickled tofu. There are also floating markets in Indonesia, Vietnam, Sri Lanka, Bangladesh, India and other South Asian countries.

★ The world's **largest fish and seafood market** is the Tsukiji Fish Market in Tokyo, Japan.

★ The world's **largest flea market** is El Rastro in Madrid, Spain.

To my amma, for her quiet strength — M. S.
For Anik, beautiful and dear soul — M. C.

The author took these photographs at the outdoor markets she often visited as a child. They were taken during her 2019 summer trip to Chennai, her hometown in southern India.

turmeric & vermilion
chili peppers

rickshaw
drums
saris
peacock feather fans

bangles
terracotta pots
vegetables
lotus buds

Barefoot Books
Bradford Mill, 23 Bradford Street, West Concord, MA 01742
29/30 Fitzroy Square, London, W1T 6LQ

Text and photographs copyright © 2020 by Meera Sriram
Illustrations copyright © 2020 by Mariona Cabassa
The moral rights of Meera Sriram and Mariona Cabassa
have been asserted

First published in the United States of America by Barefoot Books, Inc
and in Great Britain by Barefoot Books, Ltd in 2020
This paperback edition first published in 2021
All rights reserved

Graphic design by Sarah Soldano, Barefoot Books
Edited and art directed by Lisa Rosinsky and
Nivair H. Gabriel, Barefoot Books

Reproduction by Bright Arts, Hong Kong
Printed in China on 100% acid-free paper
This book was typeset in Bentham, DK Crayon Crumble and Mr. Anteater
The illustrations for this book were prepared in pencils, pastels and
water-based paints

Paperback ISBN 978-1-64686-273-3

British Cataloguing-in-Publication Data: a catalogue
record for this book is available from the British Library

Library of Congress Cataloging-in-Publication Data
is available under LCCN 2020006121

3 5 7 9 8 6 4